THIS WALKER BOOK BELONGS TO:

For Tash,
and for Stephen
P.J.L.

First published 1985 by Walker Books Ltd
87 Vauxhall Walk, London SE11 5HJ

This edition published 1999

2 4 6 8 10 9 7 5 3 1

Text © 1985 Sarah Hayes
Illustrations © 1993 P. J. Lynch

This book has been typeset in Berkeley.

Printed in Hong Kong

British Library Cataloguing in Publication Data
A catalogue record for this book is
available from the British Library.

ISBN 0-7445-6956-7

FAVOURITE FAIRY TALES

Retold by
SARAH HAYES

Illustrated by
P.J. LYNCH

WALKER BOOKS
AND SUBSIDIARIES
LONDON • BOSTON • SYDNEY

Contents

Puss in Boots

Once upon a time a poor miller died, leaving three sons. To the eldest he gave his mill, to the second his donkey and to the third he gave his cat.

"We're out of luck, Puss," said the miller's youngest son. "When the winter sets in we shall die of cold. I shall have to make you into a muff!"

Now Puss did not care for the sound of this, and spoke up. "Do not despair, Master," he said. "I can be of great service to you." The miller's son was surprised to hear his cat speak, but he listened intently to what Puss had to say.

"Just find me a good pair of boots, a hat with a plume and

a sack," said Puss. "Do as I say and your fortune is made."

The miller's son did as he was told, and Puss pulled on his boots, set the hat on his head and strode off into the woods. Soon he caught a fine big rabbit in the sack. He strode out of the woods and up the high road to the palace, where he demanded to see the king.

With a low bow and a flourish of his hat, Puss laid the sack before the king. "Sire, I bring a gift for Your Majesty from my master, the Marquis of Carabas."

"Your master is most generous," said the king, wondering who the Marquis of Carabas might be. Of course he could not know that this was just a name Puss had invented for his master.

The next day Puss caught two plump partridges in his sack, which he also presented to the king in the name of the Marquis of Carabas. "Your master is most generous," the king said again, even more curious about the mysterious Marquis of Carabas.

Week followed week, and every day Puss trapped some game and presented it to the king in the name of the Marquis of Carabas.

By and by Puss discovered that the king was to take a drive in the country with his beautiful daughter.

"Quickly, Master," said Puss. "Take off all your clothes and jump into the river. Do as I say and your fortune is made." The miller's son was a little surprised, but he did as he was told, and Puss hid his ragged clothes under a stone.

As the king's coach passed the river, Puss ran on to the road, shouting, "Help! Help! The Marquis of Carabas is drowning!"

The king recognized Puss, stopped his coach and sent his men to rescue the marquis. "Sire, I must explain," said Puss. "Robbers have stolen my master's clothes and thrown him in the river to drown."

Immediately the king sent

for a magnificent suit of clothes from his own wardrobe.

Suitably clad in the king's velvet breeches and a satin cloak, the young man looked so handsome (for he was good-looking to start with) that the princess fell quite in love with him.

Puss, meanwhile, strode on ahead to where some peasants were cutting hay.

"When the king comes along," said Puss, "you must say that all these fields belong to the Marquis of Carabas, or I'll mince you into little pieces." The peasants did as they were told, and the king was much impressed.

Puss strode on until he came to a field where more

peasants were harvesting corn. "When the king comes along," ordered Puss, "you must say that all the land round here belongs to the Marquis of Carabas, or I'll mince you into little tiny pieces." The peasants did as they were told, and the king was even more impressed.

By now Puss had reached a mighty castle belonging to the real owner of the land – an ogre. Boldly Puss demanded to see the ogre. "I have been told," said Puss, "that you have the power to transform yourself into the shape of any animal you choose, but I cannot believe it."

"It's true!" roared the ogre, changing himself into a lion. Puss was so terrified that he leapt on to the roof. He had forgotten that his boots would make him clumsy, and he almost fell off.

"I've also been told," said Puss, quaking with fear, "that you can take the shape of a very small animal such as a rat or a mouse. That I cannot believe!"

"Easy!" roared the ogre, and the roar turned to a squeak as he changed himself into a mouse.

Puss immediately pounced on the mouse and ate him up. So that was the end of the ogre.

Puss ordered the ogre's servants to prepare a great banquet, and hurried over the drawbridge just in time to meet the king, the princess and his master.

"Welcome to the castle of the Marquis of Carabas," said Puss, bowing low and waving his hat with the plume.

"Your master is obviously a man of great importance," said the king to Puss a little later, over a goblet of wine. And when the banquet was over, he offered his daughter's hand in marriage to the Marquis of Carabas.

So the princess and the poor miller's son were married and lived happily ever after. Puss gave up hunting, hung up his boots and his hat with the plume, and lived a life of luxury at the palace for many long years.

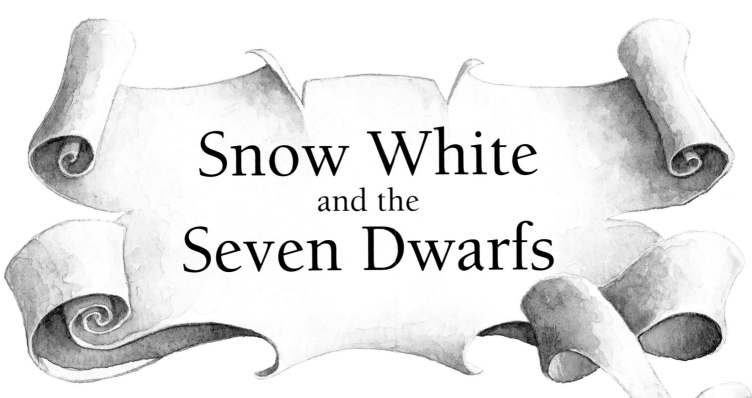

Snow White
and the
Seven Dwarfs

Once upon a time a young queen sat by a window sewing. As she gazed at the snowflakes falling, her needle slipped and pricked her finger. A drop of blood welled up. "Alas," she sighed, "how I wish I could bear a child as white as snow, and as red as blood, with hair as black as the ebony of the window frame."

A year later the young queen's wish was granted, and she gave birth to a daughter with skin as white as snow, lips as red as blood and hair as black as ebony. "Let her be called Snow White," were the queen's last words, for she died soon after the baby was born.

When Snow White was a year old, the king married

again. His new queen was beautiful, but she was proud and jealous and full of wicked schemes. She had a secret room in the castle where a magic mirror hung, and there she would stand, gazing at her reflection and saying,

"Mirror, mirror, on the wall,
Who is the fairest one of all?"

The mirror would answer,

"You, O Queen, are the fairest one."

And the queen would smile and be satisfied.

Yet every day little Snow White grew more beautiful, and the wicked queen more jealous. On the day of Snow White's fifteenth birthday, the queen once again slipped off to her secret room and stood before her magic glass.

"Mirror, mirror, on the wall,
Who is the fairest one of all?"

The mirror always spoke the truth.

"You, O Queen, have beauty rare,
But Snow White is ten times more fair."

The queen raged and fumed, hating Snow White. She called a huntsman and told him to take Snow White into the forest and kill her. "Bring me her heart so I may know she is dead," said the wicked queen.

Snow White was very frightened when the huntsman

took her deep into the forest and drew his knife. She looked up into his face and tears rolled down her cheeks. The huntsman took pity on her and told her to run off into the forest. On his way home he killed a young deer and cut out its heart to give to the queen.

The forest was dark and dangerous and full of wild beasts. Snow White ran and ran until she came to a clearing where a little cottage stood. Desperate for food and rest, she pushed open the door and entered. No one was at home, but a meal had been laid for seven people on a low table covered with a white cloth. Snow White took a taste from each of the seven bowls, hoping the owners would not notice, and took a sip from each of the seven cups. Then she tried each of the neat little beds in the bedroom. Some were too small, some were too narrow or too high, but one was perfect. Snow White soon fell fast asleep.

She did not hear the tramp, tramp of seven pairs of boots, nor the crash of seven pickaxes being thrown on the floor. The cottage belonged to seven dwarfs who spent their days mining for silver and gold in the hills beyond the forest.

"Now who's been sitting in my chair?" asked one.

"Who's been scraping my bowl?" asked another.

"Who's been supping with my spoon?" asked a third.

"Who's been cutting with my knife?" asked a fourth.

"Who's been eating my bread?" asked a fifth.

"Who's been drinking from my cup?" asked a sixth.

"And who is this, lying in my bed?" asked the seventh. The dwarfs ran to look and were so taken with Snow White's beauty that they did not want to wake her. That night, the seventh dwarf shared a bed with the others, an hour with each.

When she awoke, Snow White was alarmed by the sight of the seven little men clustered round her, but they made her so welcome that she was soon quite at home. The dwarfs were shocked at her story and made Snow White promise to stay with them.

"You can cook and clean and keep house for us," said one.

"We shall be away all day, though," said another.

"You must take great care," said a third.

"The wicked queen is sure to come and look for you," said a fourth.

"Let no one in," said a fifth.

"No one," echoed the sixth and seventh.

So Snow White kept house for the seven dwarfs, and a very merry house it was for a month or two. Then one day the wicked queen went to her secret room and looked into her magic glass.

> *"Mirror, mirror, on the wall,*
> *Who is the fairest one of all?"*

The mirror answered,

> *"You, O Queen, have beauty rare,*
> *Yet lives there one ten times more fair.*
> *In seven dwarfs' house by yonder hill,*
> *Snow White is the fairer still."*

The queen fumed and raged and plotted all night how she might kill Snow White. In the morning she painted her face and disguised herself as an old pedlar. Carrying a basket piled high with ribbons and lace and trimmings of all colours, she made her way to the seven dwarfs' cottage.

"Ribbons and laces for sale," she called. "Pretty ribbons."

Snow White looked out of the window and saw the bright colours of the pedlar's basket. She opened the door and chose a ribbon.

"Let me lace you up," said the old woman. "You can be laced properly for once." Snow White suspected nothing, and she stood quietly while the woman threaded the ribbon through once, twice, three, four times. Then she pulled the laces so tightly that Snow White could not breathe, and she fell to the floor.

"Now we shall see who is the fairest one of all," said the queen, and she hurried away.

When the seven dwarfs returned and found their dear Snow White on the ground, they were horrified. Four of them lifted her up and three cut the laces that were suffocating her. In a moment or two Snow White recovered.

"That was no pedlar," said one of the dwarfs.

"That was the wicked queen," said another.

"You must promise to let no one in while we are away," said a third sternly.

"I promise," Snow White said.

The queen meanwhile went into her secret room and stood before the magic mirror.

> *"Mirror, mirror, on the wall,*
>
> *Who is the fairest one of all?"*

The mirror answered,

> *"You, O Queen, have beauty rare,*
>
> *Yet lives there one ten times more fair.*
>
> *In seven dwarfs' house by yonder hill,*
>
> *Snow White is the fairer still."*

The queen's face grew pale with fury. Snow White was alive! All night she fumed and raged and plotted, and by morning she had made a jewelled comb so poisonous it would kill anyone who used it. Disguised as a gypsy, she made her way to the dwarfs' cottage.

"Bracelets and bows," she called. "Trinkets and combs."

Snow White looked out of the window. "I dare not let you in," she said, but the gypsy held up the comb and let the light catch the jewels. Snow White ran to open the door.

"Let me comb your hair," said the gypsy. "It is so long and beautiful." As soon as the comb touched her hair, the poison took effect and Snow White fell to the ground.

"So much for your beauty," laughed the wicked queen and she hurried back to the castle.

When the dwarfs came home, they quickly pulled out the poisoned comb and Snow White revived. This time they made Snow White swear to let no one in.

At the castle the queen stood once more before her magic mirror.

*"Mirror, mirror, on the wall,
Who is the fairest one of all?"*

The mirror answered,

*"You, O Queen,
have beauty rare,
Yet lives there one
ten times more fair.
In seven dwarfs' house
by yonder hill,
Snow White is the fairer still."*

The queen shrieked with fury. She ground her teeth with rage. All night long, she fumed and muttered and schemed. With the aid of her black arts, she made a poisoned apple, one half green, the other half rosy red, and laid it on top of a basket of apples. Then she disguised herself as an old apple seller and made her way to the dwarfs' cottage.

"Apples, red rosy apples," she called.

"I dare not come down,"

said Snow White, looking out of the window.

"Take an apple then," said the old woman, throwing her the poisoned apple.

"I dare not," said Snow White, throwing it back.

"Afraid of poison, eh?" said the old woman, and cut the apple in two. "Look, I will eat one half, and you can eat the other."

Now the apple had been so cleverly contrived that only one half was poisoned. The old woman bit into the green half, and Snow White stretched out her hand to take the rosy red half. She had hardly taken one bite before the poison began to work and she fell lifeless to the ground.

"Black as ebony, red as blood and white as death," said the wicked queen and hurried back to the castle to look into her magic mirror.

> *"Mirror, mirror, on the wall,*
> *Who is the fairest one of all?"*

The mirror answered,

> *"You, O Queen, are the fairest one."*

The queen was satisfied, for she knew that Snow White was dead at last.

When the dwarfs returned and found Snow White, they did everything they could think of to revive her.

They cut her laces, loosened her dress, combed her hair, lifted her up, poured water over her, but all was in vain. Snow White lay dead. The dwarfs lamented loud and long, for they had loved Snow White. She was so beautiful, even in death, that the dwarfs could not bear to bury her in the ground. Instead they laid her in a coffin of clear glass with a gold inscription round it that told her name and said she was a king's daughter.

They carried it to a high mountain and took turns keeping watch by it.

Five years passed, and then a king's son lost his way in the forest and had to spend the night in the dwarfs' house. He saw the glass coffin high on the mountain and was struck with Snow White's beauty, undimmed by the years that had passed. He could not bear to leave Snow White and pressed the dwarfs to give him the coffin. At first they refused, but he was so earnest that at last they agreed.

As he rode along, gazing at Snow White's face, one of the servants carrying the coffin stumbled and the piece of poisoned apple was dislodged from Snow White's throat. She opened her eyes. "Where am I?" she said.

"You are with me," said the king's son and lifted her on to his horse.

Snow White and her prince were soon married, and invitations were sent out for a grand banquet. The wicked queen put on her finest gown for the wedding feast, and smiled triumphantly at her reflection in the glass.

> *"Mirror, mirror, on the wall,*
> *Who is the fairest one of all?"*

The mirror answered,

> *"You, O Queen, have beauty rare,*
> *But the king's son's queen is ten times more fair."*

The wicked queen stormed off to the wedding. When she saw that the bride was none other than Snow White, she was transfixed with fury, unable to move. Two iron shoes were heated till they were red-hot, and the wicked queen was made to put them on and dance and dance till she dropped down dead.

The Frog Prince

There was once a princess who lived in a magnificent castle. Her rooms were piled high with jewels and finery, but of all her splendid possessions, her favourite was a simple gold ball. One day she threw the ball high in the air and it fell into a pond so deep she could not see the bottom. She sat down and wept.

"I would give anything to get back my beautiful golden ball," she sobbed. "I would give my clothes, my jewels, all my precious things."

Just then a large green frog hopped out of the pond. "What would I want with clothes and jewels and precious things?" it croaked.

"Go away, you nasty wet creature!" shrieked the princess. "You can't get my ball back."

"There you are wrong," croaked the frog. "Give me what I want and I will get your ball."

"What do you want?" asked the princess.

"Take me home with you and let me live with you. Let me eat from your golden plate and sleep in your silken bed," answered the frog.

The princess shuddered at the thought, but she agreed nevertheless. "Do you promise?" asked the frog.

"Of course," said the princess. "But do hurry!"

The frog dived down into the depths of the pool, and soon it emerged carrying the gold ball. The princess snatched it and ran off towards the castle. "What about your promise?" called the frog, but the princess ran on without turning round.

That night the princess was eating her supper with the king and queen when something came pattering up the stairs and tapped on the door. Everyone heard the words it spoke:

"Proud princess,
Bar not the door.
Remember your promise,
I ask no more."

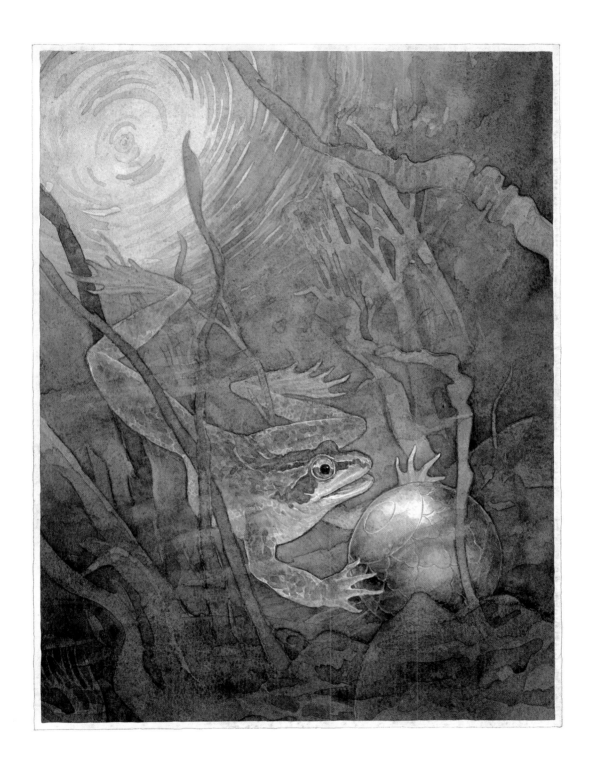

The princess opened the door and saw the frog gazing up at her. She slammed the door and ran back to the table. In a moment the tap came again, and the voice croaked,

"Proud princess,
Bar not the door.
Remember your promise,
I ask no more."

Again the princess opened the door, and again she shut it in the frog's face. When the frog spoke a third time, the king stood up. "What is the meaning of these words, daughter?" he asked. When the princess had told her story, the king frowned. "A promise is a promise, and must be kept," he said. "Let your visitor in and do as you have said you will." The princess's heart sank, but she opened the door and the frog hopped up to the table. "Put me on a stool beside you, Princess, so I may eat at your table," it said. And the princess had to do as it asked. "Push your plate a little closer so I may share your supper." The princess did this and the frog ate. The princess touched nothing.

"Now I am tired," croaked the frog. "Take me to your silken bed."

The princess began to cry, but the king said again, "A promise is a promise, and must be kept." The sobbing princess picked up the frog and carried it to her bedroom. She set it down in the furthest corner and slipped into bed.

Soon she heard a pattering on the floor and the familiar croaking voice. "A frog needs sleep the same as a princess," it said. "Put me on your silken pillow so I may share your bed."

The princess did as the frog asked. Then she turned over and cried herself to sleep.

In the morning, when she awoke, she was surprised to see a handsome prince standing beside her bed. "I was bewitched," he said, "and doomed to stay in the shape of a frog until a princess let me come into her home, and eat from her plate, and sleep in her bed."

The princess remembered how rude she had been to the frog and she felt ashamed. But she and the prince were soon married, and they lived happily for many years.

Hansel and Gretel

Once upon a time two children called Hansel and Gretel lived in the forest with their father and stepmother. Their father was a woodcutter, and he was always poor. But one winter he became poorer than ever.

"We cannot even feed Hansel and Gretel properly," he said to his wife one night.

"Why bother to feed them when we can't feed ourselves?" said his wife. "We could leave them in the forest. They would never find the way back."

The woodcutter was horrified by this idea, but his wife was cruel and strong-willed and eventually he was forced to agree. Fortunately hunger had kept Hansel and Gretel awake and they had overheard their parents talking.

"Do not worry, sister," said Hansel. "I have a plan." He slipped out of the house and gathered a pocketful of white pebbles.

In the morning the woodcutter and his wife gave the children a crust of bread and took them into the forest. Every so often Hansel stopped and looked back at the house.

"What can you see, boy?" asked his stepmother.

"I can see my little white cat on the roof, Mother," replied Hansel.

"Nonsense," snapped the stepmother. "All you can see is sunshine on the chimney-pot." But Hansel saw neither cat nor chimney-pot, for he had only turned round to throw down a pebble from his pocket.

Soon they were deep in the forest. The woodcutter built a fire and told the children to wait while he and his wife went away to chop wood. Hansel and Gretel waited and waited but no one came back. Night fell and wolves began to howl.

"Do not be afraid, sister," said Hansel. "The moon will be out soon and we will find our way home."

When the moon rose, the white pebbles gleamed like silver coins and guided the children back to their house.

The woodcutter was amazed and overjoyed when the children returned, but his wife was furious. She had failed once to get rid of the children but she would not fail again.

In the morning, for the second time, the woodcutter and his wife led the children deep into the forest. Hansel stopped every so often to look back at the house.

"What can you see, boy?" asked his stepmother.

"I can see my little white pigeon on the roof, Mother," said Hansel.

"Nonsense," snapped his stepmother. "All you can see is sunshine on the chimney-pot."

But Hansel saw neither pigeon nor chimney-pot, for he had only turned round to drop crumbs from the crust his father had given him.

Again the children were left to wait by the fire, and again the wolves began to howl as night fell. But when the moon rose, no crumbs gleamed to guide the children home, for birds had eaten them.

For two days Hansel and Gretel wandered in the forest looking for the way home. There were only berries to eat, and at night they sheltered wherever they could, hoping the wolves would not find them. On the third day, weak with hunger, they saw a beautiful snow-white bird and followed it. As they stumbled into a clearing, they saw in front of them a house made of gingerbread. The roof was sponge cake, the chimneys were twisted sugar canes, and the windows were made of sugar baked as clear as glass.

Hansel rushed forward and broke off a piece of the roof. As he ate it a little voice sang out,

"Nibble, nibble, little mouse,
Who's that nibbling at my house?"

Hansel answered,

"Do not fear, no mouse is near.

It is only the wind in the trees you hear."

He broke off another piece of the roof while Gretel pulled out a window-pane and started eating it.

Just then the door of the little house opened and out came an old woman. She smiled at the children and beckoned to them. "Come in, come in, little mice," she said. "Stay with me awhile. I have good food to eat, and comfortable beds for you to sleep in." Hansel and Gretel were happy to go inside, and after they had eaten they fell into bed and went straight to sleep.

The old woman crept upstairs to look at the sleeping children. She touched Hansel's rosy cheek. "Yes, I shall have that one first," she said and cackled softly, for she was really a horrible witch who lured little children to her house and ate them.

In the morning the witch locked Hansel in a cage and ordered Gretel to cook him a meal. "We must fatten that one up," she said, so Hansel dined like a king while Gretel ate only scraps.

Every day the witch went to the cage and asked Hansel to put out a finger so she could feel how fat he was getting.

She was very short-sighted, and every day Hansel put out a little bone for her to feel. After a month the witch grew impatient. "Fat or not, that one is for the pot," she said and ordered Gretel to build a fire for the oven. Then she asked Gretel to climb into the oven to see if it was hot. Gretel saw that the witch meant to slam the door and roast her at the same time as her brother, so she pretended not to understand.

"But how do I open the door?" she asked.

"Like this," said the witch, and showed her.

"But how do I climb in?" asked Gretel.

"Climb in like this," said the witch, and she crawled into the oven.

At once Gretel slammed the door and the witch was burnt to death.

"The witch is dead, the witch is dead, the wicked witch is dead!" sang Gretel as she ran to release Hansel from the cage. The children snatched up a bag of the witch's gold and ran away from the house as fast as they could.

Before long they had run right through the forest and back home. The woodcutter cried with joy when he saw them, and his wife could say nothing at all – for she was dead and buried long since, which was good enough for her.

The Six Swans

There was once a king who lost his way in the forest and feared he would die if he did not find a way out before nightfall. He was about to give up hope when an old woman appeared. "I will show you the path if you marry my daughter," she said. As the king's first wife was dead and the old woman's daughter was very beautiful, the king agreed. But when he arrived home with his new wife, he discovered his mistake. The woman was a witch and the new queen had inherited all her mother's evil ways.

The king already had seven children – six sons, and a daughter who bore a golden star on her forehead. Fearing that the witch-queen might do them some harm, he ordered his servant to hide the children in the forest. When he wished to visit them, he took out a magic ball of wool which unrolled and led him to the children's hiding place.

Soon the king was spending nearly all his time with the children and the witch-queen became suspicious. One day she stole the ball of wool and found the way to the children's house. The boys thought their father had arrived and ran forward to meet him. But as they did so, the witch-queen grabbed them and pulled magic shirts over their heads. Into each shirt she had

woven a wicked spell which
turned the princes into swans.
The great birds struggled and
flapped in her arms and then flew
off. When there were six swans in
the sky, the witch-queen went away.

A little later the princess with the
golden star came out of the house
to call her brothers for supper.
She called and called,
but no one came.
For three days she
wandered in the forest
calling and searching.
On the evening of the
third day she came
to a little hut on the far side
of the forest. As she sat down to rest she heard the beating
of wings, and six swans flew through the window and
landed in front of her. In a moment the six princes had
stripped off their swan skins and now stood before their
sister.

"We cannot stay princes for long," they told her. "For

fifteen minutes every day we regain our rightful shape, and then we must turn back into swans."

"How can I break this dreadful spell?" asked the princess.

"It is too much to ask," said the brothers.

"Ask it," implored the princess, and her brothers told her what she had to do.

"For six years you must never speak, and each year you must weave a shirt of star-flowers, one for each of us."

"That is not too much to ask," said the princess quietly. The princes turned back into swans and flew away.

For a year the princess searched for star-flowers. She found just enough to make one shirt. The leaves hurt her hands as she sewed, but she never made a sound. In two years she had made two shirts. Towards the end of the third year a young king who was out hunting saw the princess hiding in a tree.

"Come down!" he cried, but the princess said nothing and threw down her gold necklace.

"Come down!" he cried again. Still the princess said nothing and threw down her golden belt. Then the king sent his huntsman up to fetch her. Never a word did she speak, but the king fell in love with her all the same and brought her to his palace to be queen.

Now the king's mother was jealous of the young queen with the golden star on her forehead. When a princess was born, the king's mother stole away the baby and said that the star-queen had killed it.  The king was angry with his mother and said that his star-queen was too gentle ever to have done such a horrible deed.

When a second child was born, the king's mother again stole away the baby, and blamed the young queen.

Again the king was angry with his mother. He knew that his star-queen was innocent and would prove it if only she could speak.

When a third child was born, the king's mother again stole away the baby. This time she put a drop of blood on the star-queen's dress and the king was made to believe that his wife really had killed the baby. "She will be burnt alive," he said. And still the star-queen never said a word.

By now, six years had almost passed. Five shirts of star-flowers had been made, and as the fire was being built the young queen sewed and sewed at the sixth. Soon she had finished it, except for one sleeve.

The star-queen was brought out and the fire was lit. The flames began to crackle and rise high in the air. Then a beating of wings was heard and six swans flew out of the forest. As they swooped down to untie the queen, she threw a star-flower shirt over each of their heads. Instantly six princes stood before the king. But in place of an arm, the youngest prince had the great white wing of a swan.

At last the star-queen could speak, and she told the king of her brothers' enchantment and of the lies his mother had told. The king soon found out where his mother had hidden the three children, and then he ordered her to be put on the fire and burnt to ashes.

As for the star-queen, she lived happily with her husband, her children and her six brothers until the end of her days.

The Twelve Dancing Princesses

There was once a king who had twelve beautiful daughters. They all slept in one room, in twelve beds set side by side. Every night the king came and locked them in. But every morning, when the door was unlocked, twelve pairs of dancing shoes were found under their beds, quite worn out.

After a while the king grew very angry at having to buy so many pairs of new shoes, and he made an announcement. "Any man who discovers the secret of where the princesses go at night shall have one of my daughters in marriage and my kingdom when I am gone. But anyone who fails after three nights will be punished by death."

The first person to try was a prince. As soon as he sat down in the room with the twelve beds, the prince's eyelids began to droop. He tried and tried to stay awake, but in less than a minute he was fast asleep. And when the door was unlocked in the morning, twelve pairs of dancing shoes were found under the beds, quite worn out. The prince had no idea how they got there. The same thing happened the next night and the next, and after three nights the prince was put to death.

After that, many young men came to try their luck, but not one of them managed to stay awake and find out

where the princesses went at night. Then, one day, a soldier came to the kingdom on his way home from the wars. As he walked through the forest near the king's castle, he met a little old woman who asked him where he was going.

"I don't know exactly, ma'am," said the soldier politely. "I've had enough of fighting, but I'm not ready to settle down just yet. I thought I might visit those twelve dancing princesses and try my luck."

"You'll need more than luck," said the little old woman. "Listen carefully: after the king has locked you in with the princesses, one of them will offer you a glass of wine, but you must only pretend to drink it, and then to fall into a deep sleep." The old woman pulled a soft grey cloak from her bag. "This will make you invisible," she said. "Wear it and you'll be able to follow the princesses wherever they go."

The soldier took the cloak and put it into his rucksack. He looked round to thank the old woman, but found he was alone. When he reached the castle, everything happened exactly as she had said it would. As soon as the king had turned the key in the lock, the eldest princess gave the soldier a goblet of wine. He poured it away when no one was looking. Then he sat down in a chair and started to yawn. In a few minutes he was snoring loudly.

The eldest princess looked down at him. The soldier kept his eyes tightly closed. "Just like all the others," said the eldest princess scornfully. Then she went to a tall cupboard and got out her dancing dress and her new dancing shoes. So did all the other princesses. The youngest princess was very slow getting ready. "Something's wrong," she said.

"Nonsense," said the eldest princess. "You're always afraid." Then she clapped her hands and her bed sank into the floor, revealing a flight of steps which led underground. One by one the princesses disappeared down the steps, and when the last one had gone, the soldier jumped up, put on the little old woman's cloak and followed.

Halfway down the steps, the soldier trod on the hem of the youngest princess's dress.

"Someone pulled my dress," she screamed.

"Nonsense," said the eldest princess. "There's no one here. You must have caught your dress on a nail."

At the foot of the stairs a door opened, and the invisible soldier followed the twelve princesses down a shimmering avenue of trees. When he looked closely the soldier found the leaves were all made of silver. He broke off a twig – crack!

"What's that?" screamed the youngest princess.

"A cannon firing to welcome us," said the eldest princess, and she led the way down another avenue where the leaves were all of pure gold and another where the leaves were all of glittering diamonds. Each time the soldier picked a twig to take home and each time the youngest princess screamed as the twig broke off – crack!

At last they came to a lake where twelve boats lay waiting with twelve handsome princes to pole the princesses across.

The invisible soldier climbed into the youngest princess's boat. Halfway across the handsome prince sighed. "The boat seems very heavy and slow tonight," he said.

"It's only the heat," said the youngest princess, but she was afraid just the same.

When they reached the far side of the lake, they went into a castle where music was playing. Then they began to dance. Round and round they danced, the twelve dancing princesses and the twelve handsome princes. And round and round the invisible soldier danced, all on his own. Whenever one of the princesses tried to drink from the golden goblets, the soldier would snatch the goblet out of her hand and drink it himself. The youngest princess shivered, but her sisters didn't seem to notice.

By three o'clock in the morning the princesses' shoes were all worn out with dancing, so the handsome princes poled them back across the lake. This time the soldier sat in the eldest princess's boat. And when they ran home, the soldier stayed close to the eldest princess, down the avenue of trees with glittering diamond leaves, down the avenue of trees with pure gold leaves, down the avenue of trees with shimmering silver leaves, and up the steps into

the princesses' bedroom. The soldier ran ahead and threw himself into his chair.

"We're quite safe," said the eldest princess when she heard the soldier's snores. She clapped her hands and the bed came up out of the floor. Then the princesses put away their dancing dresses, threw their worn-out shoes under their beds and went to sleep.

The soldier said nothing when the king came to unlock the door in the morning. But he followed the princesses the next night and the next. Everything happened just as it had before. On the third and last night, the soldier took one of the golden goblets from the castle. And when the king came to unlock the door, the soldier told him everything that had happened. He showed him the twigs with leaves of silver, gold and diamonds. He showed him the golden goblet.

"But how do my daughters' shoes get all worn out?" asked the king.

"By dancing the night away with twelve handsome princes who live in an underground castle on the far side of an underground lake," replied the soldier.

Then the princesses knew their secret was discovered and the soldier could choose any one of them to be his wife.

"Which is it to be?" asked the king.

"I'm not a young man," said the soldier, "so I'll take the eldest." And so he did. And when the king died, the soldier became king and ruled very well.

But what happened to the eleven dancing princesses and the twelve handsome princes who lived in the underground castle on the far side of the underground lake no one ever knew.

Sleeping Beauty

Once upon a time there lived a king and queen who were very unhappy because they had no children. After many years, when they had almost given up hope, the queen gave birth to a beautiful daughter.

A grand christening was arranged, and seven fairies were asked to be godmothers to the baby princess. At the magnificent christening feast, seven places of honour were laid for the seven godmothers. In front of each fairy stood a gold goblet studded with rubies and diamonds and a gold knife, fork and spoon.

As the guests sat down to dinner, a mumbling and a muttering was heard outside the hall. In hobbled an ancient

fairy, in a temper as black as thunder. She lived in a high tower in the castle and had not been seen for fifty years. The king, the queen and everyone in the castle had forgotten all about her.

A place was hastily laid, but there was no gold goblet or knife, fork and spoon for the aged fairy, and she had to make do with silver. She sat down muttering words of revenge under her breath. A young fairy who was sitting nearby heard these threats and feared for the princess's safety. So while the other godmothers gathered to present their gifts, the young fairy crept behind the curtains. One by one the fairies gave their gifts to the princess.

The first gave the gift of beauty; the second gave good nature; the third the gift of grace; the fourth the art of dancing; the fifth said the princess would sing like a nightingale; and the sixth that she would be able to play any musical instrument she chose. Then, shaking with fury, the aged fairy stood up and pointed a bony finger at the baby in the cradle. "My gift to the princess is this," she said. "When she reaches her sixteenth birthday, the princess will prick her finger on a spindle and die!" A gasp of horror ran round the court. Then the young fairy stepped out from behind the curtains.

"I have not the power to undo this evil spell," said she, "but my gift to the princess is this: when she reaches her sixteenth birthday, she will indeed prick her finger, but she will not die. Instead she will go to sleep for a hundred years, and then a prince will come and wake her."

The princess grew up to be as beautiful as the fairies had wished. The king banned all spindles and spinning wheels throughout the land, and the wicked fairy's spell was quite forgotten until the day of the princess's sixteenth birthday.

The princess was wandering through the castle when she discovered a little winding staircase she had not seen before. At the top of the stairs she found a room where an old woman sat spinning. The woman had never heard the proclamation banning spinning wheels.

The princess watched the spindle spin round and listened to the whirr of the wheel. "Oh, please may I try?" she asked, but no sooner had she taken hold of the thread than the spindle pricked her finger and she fell to the ground.

Horrified, the old woman called for help. People came running but none could revive the princess, who lay

fast asleep, a slight smile on her lips. The king ordered a great bed to be made, hung with tapestries embroidered in gold and silver. The young fairy was summoned, but there was nothing she could do. When she saw the sleeping princess lying on her great gold and silver bed, she was concerned. "How frightened the princess will be," she said to herself, "when she wakes up in a hundred years and finds herself alone and everything changed." So the fairy made sure that nothing would change. She went from room to room touching everyone and everything with her wand. Ladies dressing, gentlemen drinking, soldiers on guard, cooks rolling pastry, boys turning spits, cats about to pounce, horses kicking stable doors – all fell into a deep sleep at a touch of the wand. Even the princess's little spaniel lay snoring at the foot of the gold and silver bed.

Years passed, and a great forest of tangled bushes and thorns grew up around the castle and hid it from view. No one went near. People forgot about the sleeping princess.

After a hundred years, a young prince who was out hunting saw the sun glinting on the towers of a far-off castle. "Whose castle is that?" he asked his huntsmen, but none knew. Then he asked the peasants who lived nearby. One said the castle was haunted, another that it was the

home of a witch, a third that it belonged to an ogre who ate little children for breakfast. Then a very old man came forward and told a tale his father's father had told, a tale of a sleeping princess.

The prince was determined to find out the truth for himself, and he drew his sword ready to hack down the tangle of thorns which surrounded the castle. But miraculously the branches drew back at his approach and the thorns turned aside, only to close in again as he passed, so that no one could follow. The prince walked on through the hedge of briars until he reached a vast courtyard filled with people so still he thought they were dead, but then he saw they were breathing.

On went the prince through the castle and up the stairs to the room with the gold and silver bed. There he saw the princess, and as he knelt down to kiss her, she opened her eyes and said, "At last my prince has come. How long you have kept me waiting!"

The prince was so overcome he didn't know what to say. But the princess could hardly stop talking, and while she talked people all over the castle began to wake up and go about their business. The prince and princess were married that very day and lived happily ever after.

Rapunzel

There was once a poor peasant who lived next door to a witch. He and his wife longed for a child, and eventually their wish was granted. As the day drew near for the baby to be born, the peasant's wife began to spend all her time gazing at the vegetables in the witch's garden. At last she could stand it no longer.

"Husband!" she cried. "You must fetch me some of the rampion which grows in the witch's garden, or I shall die." The peasant looked at his wife and saw how pale she had become, and he knew she spoke the truth. When it was dark, he climbed over the high wall and dropped into the witch's garden. He quickly dug up a few rampion roots, which he took back for his wife. She ate the rampion greedily, and by morning she was asking for more. This time the witch was waiting in her garden when the peasant climbed over the wall.

"He who steals my rampion will pay for it with his life!" shrieked the witch.

"It is f-for my w-wife," stammered the peasant. "She will die without it, and the baby too."

The witch thought for a moment. "Give me your baby and I shall spare your life." The peasant was so terrified that he agreed, and as soon as the baby was born, the witch came and took it away. She called the baby Rapunzel after the rampion the peasant had stolen from her garden.

Rapunzel grew up to be a beautiful girl with very long golden hair. On the day of her twelfth birthday, she was taken into the forest by the witch and shut up in a high tower which had neither a door nor stairs. Whenever the witch wanted to go to Rapunzel's room, she stood at the foot of the tower and said,

"Rapunzel, Rapunzel,
Let down your hair."

Then Rapunzel let her hair hang down from the window, and the witch grabbed hold of it and clambered up the wall.

Rapunzel was often lonely in her room, and sometimes she would gaze out across the forest and sing sad songs. One day a king's son was out hunting when he heard the beautiful sad singing and rode towards it. He looked up at the tower, but he could not see Rapunzel's face, for the window was too high. He searched in vain for a door or a stairway and vowed he would return the following day.

True to his word, he came the next day, and the next. On the third day the king's son saw the witch arrive at the tower, and he quickly hid behind a tree. He heard the witch call for Rapunzel, and watched the golden hair come tumbling down and the witch go climbing up. He waited until the witch had gone, and then he came to the foot of the tower.

"Rapunzel, Rapunzel,
Let down your hair!"

he cried, and the golden hair came tumbling down. In a moment he had climbed up the tower and entered Rapunzel's room.

Rapunzel was very frightened at first, for she had never seen a man before. But the king's son visited her every day, and soon she fell in love with him. Every time he came, the king's son brought a skein of silk. And while the witch was away, Rapunzel sewed the silk to make a ladder so that she could escape from the tower and marry the king's son. Soon the ladder was nearly finished, and Rapunzel could think of nothing but her escape. One day she said to the witch without thinking, "Why is it that you take so long to climb the tower? The king's son is with me in an instant."

Then the witch knew that the king's son had been to visit Rapunzel, and she was furious. She took a pair of scissors and cut off all Rapunzel's golden hair.

Then she sent her away to wander in the desert. She fastened the hair to the window-sill and sat down to wait. Towards evening the king's son arrived and cried out,

"Rapunzel, Rapunzel,
Let down your hair!"

The witch threw the golden hair out of the window and in an instant the king's son was up the tower. When he reached the window, there, to his horror, was the witch, who shrieked out,

*"Your singing bird
Has flown the nest.
Cat got her first;
Your eyes are next!"*
The king's son was so
overcome with grief that he
threw himself out of the
window. He fell on to a thorn-
bush, which scratched his
eyes and blinded him. For a
year he wandered sorrowfully
about the world until one day
he came to a desert and heard
the sweet sad voice of
Rapunzel, whom he thought
was dead. When she saw his
poor blind eyes, Rapunzel
began to weep. And as her
tears fell on his eyes, the
king's son began to see again.

Rapunzel and he were
soon married, and they lived
happily ever after.

Beauty
and the
Beast

O nce upon a time there was a rich merchant who had three daughters. The youngest and prettiest was called Beauty. She had a kind heart, and everyone loved her except her jealous sisters.

One winter there was a terrible storm at sea and the merchant lost all of his ships. He had to sell his fine town house and move into a little cottage in the country. The two older daughters wept and grumbled. They stayed in bed all day, bewailing the loss of their fine clothes, but Beauty rose at four every morning to cook and keep house for her father.

Then one day the merchant heard that one of his ships had survived the storm, and at once he got ready to go to the town.

"Bring me back a fur cape," said the eldest daughter as her father was setting out.

"And bring me a silk gown," said the second daughter.

"And I want a hat with ribbons," added the eldest.

"But what does Beauty want?" interrupted the merchant.

"Bring me a rose, Father," said Beauty. She wanted nothing more than her father's safe return, but she knew her sisters would tease her if she said that.

The merchant spent three days in the town sorting out his business. But in the end he was no richer than before. As he rode home, snow began to fall and soon he realized he was lost. He wandered about for hours until he found himself in an avenue of trees which led to the door of a great house.

Before he had time to knock, the door opened by itself.

Inside the merchant could see a hall with marble pillars. At one end a huge fire blazed and a table was laid for supper. The merchant entered and stood by the fire, waiting for the owner of the house to appear. He waited and waited but no one came, so at last he sat down to eat. After supper he went upstairs and at once found a bedroom where the bed had already been made for him, and the covers turned back. Gratefully he lay down and slept.

In the morning he looked out of the window and saw that all the snow had melted. A garden full of roses stretched down to the banks of a stream. This wonderful place must belong to some good fairy, he thought. Then he said out loud, "I thank you for your kindness and hospitality, Fairy, but now I must be on my way."

As he walked through the rose garden, the merchant remembered Beauty's request and he broke off a spray of white roses. Immediately there was a noise like thunder, and a hideous beast sprang from the bushes.

"Ungrateful man!" roared the beast. "I give you food and shelter and this is how you repay me. You steal the thing I love most in the world.

Your punishment is death!"

The merchant was terrified. "Forgive me, Lord, I did not mean to steal. I only wanted a rose to give to my youngest daughter."

"Do not call me Lord," growled the beast, "call me Beast, for that is what I am. Listen, Merchant. I will strike a bargain with you. If one of your daughters comes to stay with me of her own free will, I will spare your life." The merchant did not like the bargain, but reluctantly he agreed and rode home with a heavy heart.

When they heard his story, the older daughters flew into a fury and said it was all Beauty's fault for asking for something so stupid as a rose. Beauty wept and said she would rather die herself than cause her father's death. So the following day the merchant and Beauty took the road back to the Beast's house.

When they arrived, everything happened as before. The door opened by itself; fires were blazing in every room; supper was laid in the marble hall. And after they had dined, a roar announced the arrival of the Beast.

"Have you come here of your own free will?" the Beast asked Beauty.

"Yes, Beast," she answered, hardly daring to look at him.

"Very well," said the Beast. "Merchant, you must leave tomorrow and never come here again. Good night, Beauty."

"Good night," said Beauty, and the Beast disappeared.

When Beauty was ready for bed, she found a door with her name painted in gold. Inside was a suite of rooms with books, a harpsichord and a wardrobe of sumptuous clothes. On one wall hung a magic mirror which showed Beauty all that was happening at home. At this moment she could see her sisters laughing together at her misfortune. She turned away and opened a book. Letters of gold blazed out:

WELCOME, BEAUTY, DO NOT FEAR,

YOU ARE QUEEN AND MISTRESS HERE.

The following morning Beauty woke to find clothes laid out for her and breakfast waiting. After her father had left, she went out into the garden and wandered there all day long. Not a soul did she see until nine o'clock, when she sat down for supper. Then she heard a roar, and the Beast appeared.

"Do you mind if I watch you eat?" he asked in the gentlest voice he could manage.

"No, Beast," said Beauty.

"Do you find me truly hideous?" he asked.

Beauty looked closely at him for the first time.

"Yes," she said, and turned away, for she hated to hurt his feelings. "But you are truly kind-hearted."

"What use is a kind heart?" the Beast sighed, making Beauty feel such pity that she quite forgot her fear.

The evening passed and when midnight struck, the Beast asked Beauty to be his wife. Beauty could not conceal her horror.

"No, Beast," she replied at last, and the Beast groaned and disappeared.

As day followed day and the days turned into weeks, Beauty began to enjoy her solitary life at the great house. Everything she could ever want was provided, and she even began to look forward to her evenings with the Beast. But every night he asked her to be his wife, and every night she answered sadly, "No, Beast." She did not like to make him sad, but she knew she could never marry him.

One day Beauty looked into her magic mirror and saw that her father had become ill with grief and worry. That evening she spoke to the Beast. "I will not marry you, Beast, for I can only love you as a friend, not as a wife." The Beast groaned, but Beauty continued. "I have decided to stay here with you always, but first let me visit my father, for he is ill and he needs me."

The Beast agreed, but he made Beauty promise to stay away no longer than a week. He gave her a ring with a milk-white stone and said, "When you wish to return, put this ring by your bedside and you will be back here in the morning. But be sure to appear in one week's time, or I shall die of sorrow."

When Beauty arrived home, her father was overjoyed and his happiness soon made him well again, but her sisters were as miserable as ever. One had married a clever man who sneered at his foolish wife, and the other had a husband who thought only of himself.

Beauty felt sorry for them and wanted to give them some of her beautiful dresses. But when she went to open the chest containing the dresses, it flew out of the window. "Oh, Beast," she sighed, "I see you intend these dresses for me alone." The chest reappeared. "You think only of me, Beast," she continued. "You are so good and kind. Even if I don't really love you, why should I not marry you?"

Beauty resolved to accept the Beast's offer of marriage on her return, but her sisters were envious of her wealth and happiness, and they decided to make her break her promise to the Beast. When it was time for Beauty to go, they threw such a fit of weeping and wailing that she was forced to say that she would stay for another week.

That night Beauty dreamt that she saw the Beast lying by the stream in his garden. The look of anguish and reproach upon his dear face was so pitiful that she woke up in tears. She placed the ring by her bedside and in the morning found herself back in her bedroom in the Beast's house.

She dressed herself in her richest gown and waited eagerly for night to come. When the clock struck nine and no Beast appeared, she became alarmed. She looked in all the rooms of the great house, calling his name. She ran out on to the terrace, past the fountains, through the rose arbour, under the great arch of trees. Then she saw him lying by the stream, just as he had appeared in her dream, and it was plain that he was dead, or dying.

Beauty ran to him and sprinkled water on his face. The Beast's eyes flickered open. "You broke your promise," he said, "and I must die. But now I shall at least die happy."

"You must not die, Beast!" cried Beauty. "Live and let me be your wife!"

As she spoke, the sky was set alight with fireworks. For a moment Beauty was dazzled, but when she could see clearly again, a handsome young man stood before her. The Beast was nowhere to be seen.

"I was once your Beast," said the young man. "By coming to me freely and promising to be my wife, you have broken the spell that bound me. Now I am a prince again."

Beauty and her prince were soon married and lived happily ever after. As for the jealous sisters, they were turned into statues which stood in front of the prince's house and frightened away the pigeons.

Cinderella

Once there was a merchant who decided to marry again. His first wife had died long ago, and he felt that his only daughter needed a mother. But his second wife was very different from the first. She was proud and bossy, and she had two daughters who were exactly like her. The merchant's daughter was kind and gentle, which infuriated her stepmother because it showed up the bad manners of her own daughters.

The stepmother did everything she could to make her stepdaughter's life a misery. The poor girl was made to wash the clothes, scrub the floors, do the dishes and sweep the stairs. She slept on a straw mattress in the attic, while

her stepsisters had grand rooms with four-poster beds and mirrors from floor to ceiling. At the end of the day she would creep into the seat in the chimney corner and warm herself by the cinders of the fire. Javotte, the elder stepsister, used to call her Cinderkin, but Claudette, the younger sister, called her Cinderella, and this became her name.

The merchant was afraid of his new wife, and Cinderella knew that if she complained it would only make him unhappy, so she never said a word. As the weeks passed, her clothes grew more and more ragged and her hands became rough, but she still remained a thousand times more beautiful than her sisters.

One morning Cinderella came downstairs to find the household in an uproar. The king was giving a grand ball for his son and everyone of any importance had been invited. The stepsisters were quarrelling about what they were going to wear.

"I think I shall wear my red brocade with the lace edging," said Claudette. "Cinderella, this lace needs mending."

Javotte was holding up a flounced petticoat covered in bows. "I've only got this old petticoat," she wailed. "But my new gold cape can go over it, and I could wear my diamond necklace."

"But what about my hair?" shrieked Claudette. "Cinderella, my hair!" Wearily Cinderella picked up the clothes her sisters had dropped. Then she began to brush Claudette's hair.

"And what will you wear for the ball, Cinderella?" asked Javotte. The stepsisters began to titter. "Rags and tatters are all the rage," said Claudette.

"You are teasing me, Sisters," said Cinderella quietly. "How can I go to the ball?"

"How can you indeed?" replied Claudette.
"Go fetch my patches instead, and be quick about it."

"No, no, find my curl-papers!" cried Javotte, and the sisters began to squabble again.

For two days Cinderella fetched and carried for the sisters and bore all their rudeness and ill temper without complaint. But when she had waved off the carriage which had been hired to take her father and sisters to the ball, she sat down in the chimney corner and wept. "How I wish … I wish…" she sobbed.

"You wish you could go to the ball, and so you shall," said a voice close by. Cinderella looked up and saw an old woman, leaning on a stick. "I am your fairy godmother and this stick is my wand," she said. "Now be a good girl and bring me a pumpkin from the garden."

Cinderella was too surprised to reply, but she did as she was told and soon found a fine big pumpkin. The old woman tapped it with her stick. With a flash, the pumpkin changed into a magnificent golden coach.

"Now fetch me the mousetrap from the stables," said the old woman. In a minute Cinderella was back with the trap, which held six scurrying grey mice. As each mouse came out of the trap, the old woman tapped it on the nose and

turned it into a horse. Soon six dappled coach horses of an elegant grey stood pawing the ground before her.

"Now for the coachman," said the old woman. "Find me the rat trap." There were three fat rats in the trap. The old woman chose the one with the longest whiskers. She tapped him on the nose with her stick and up stood a fat coachman with a long curly moustache.

Then the old woman thought for a moment. "Ah yes, I remember," she said quietly. "My dear, you will find six lizards behind the water tank. Bring them here." With a tap of the wand she turned the lizards into six footmen stiff with gold braid. "That will do," she said, putting down her stick.

Cinderella looked down at her tattered dress. "But, Godmother, I have no proper clothes," she said. The old woman smiled and waved her wand once more. Instantly, Cinderella's rags were changed into a sumptuous gown of pink velvet studded with sapphires. On her head she had a silver circlet set with diamonds and on her feet a pair of tiny slippers made entirely of glass.

"Now you may go to the ball, my dear," said the old woman. "But do not stay later than midnight. When the clock strikes twelve, your coach will turn back into a pumpkin and you will be Cinderella again."

The ball had already begun when Cinderella arrived. As she entered the ballroom, with a footman holding the train of her dress, all eyes turned to look at her. The orchestra stopped playing. The prince had never seen such a beautiful girl. He stepped forward and asked her to dance. The room began to hum with questions: Who was she? What was her name? Was she a princess? Who dressed her hair? Who made her gown?

For the rest of the evening the prince danced with Cinderella. She left his side only once, to speak to her stepsisters, who blushed and giggled and curtseyed far too often. Not for one moment did Claudette and Javotte suspect that the beautiful princess was their own bedraggled little stepsister.

At a quarter to midnight Cinderella slipped away from the ball. On the last stroke of twelve the ball gown, coach, horses, coachman and footmen all changed back into the things they had been before. When the sisters returned home, they found Cinderella in her usual seat in the chimney corner.

Claudette and Javotte spoke of nothing but the unknown princess: how beautiful she was, how taken the prince had been with her and how gracious she had been to them in particular. "What was her name?" asked Cinderella.

"That was the odd thing," said Claudette. "No one seemed to know." Cinderella smiled and climbed the stairs to her attic bedroom.

The following day a second ball was announced, for the prince longed to see the unknown princess again. This time the fairy godmother gave Cinderella a dress made of silver studded with pearls. Again she arrived late at the ball, and again the prince danced with no one else. The hours passed so quickly that it was almost midnight before Cinderella left. Her clothes had turned to rags before she reached home.

The following day the prince announced a third ball, and this time the old woman gave Cinderella a dress of gold set with diamonds. Everything happened as before, but Cinderella forgot to look at the time and suddenly she heard the clock beginning to strike twelve. She tore herself

from the prince's arms and ran out of the ballroom. As she hurried down the steps, one of the glass slippers came off, but she could not stop to pick it up and ran on towards the palace gate.

When the prince asked the guards at the gate if they had seen the princess's coach departing, all they could do was shake their heads. The only person they had seen was a peasant girl running along with a pumpkin and a cage of mice in her arms.

The prince was in despair. He sat up all night gazing at the glass slipper. In the morning he summoned all the princesses in the land to come and try on the slipper; then all the duchesses and viscountesses; then all the ladies of the court. The glass slipper did not fit any of them. The prince ordered his chamberlain to search the town; every house was to be visited and every girl asked to try on the slipper.

When the chamberlain arrived at Cinderella's house, the stepsisters pushed and jostled to be the first to try on the slipper. Claudette curled up her toes, but her feet were far too long. Javotte pinched her heels, but her feet were far too broad.

"Is that your other daughter?" the chamberlain asked the merchant.

"Oh, she's only a cinderkin," said Javotte before her father could reply.

"Hardly more than a servant," added Claudette. But the chamberlain had noticed the beauty of the girl who sat in the chimney corner in rags. He handed Cinderella the slipper and she put it on.

It fitted perfectly. Cinderella put her hand in her apron pocket and drew out the other slipper. At that moment her fairy godmother appeared and touched Cinderella with her wand, turning her rags into a dress of white silk woven with moonbeams. Claudette and Javotte fell at her feet and begged for forgiveness.

Now Cinderella was as kind and generous as she was beautiful, so she immediately forgave her sisters. What is more, she found husbands for them from the gentlemen of the court. As for Cinderella herself, she and the prince were married that day, and they lived happily ever after.

MORE WALKER PAPERBACKS
For You to Enjoy

Also illustrated by P. J. Lynch

EAST O' THE SUN AND WEST O' THE MOON
by Naomi Lewis

Shortlisted for the Kate Greenaway Medal

A stunning edition of a classic, romantic Norwegian fairy tale – a kind of *Beauty and the Beast* with magic and mystery, a curse and a quest, and trolls with some of the longest noses ever seen!

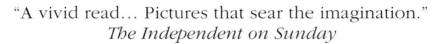

"A vivid read… Pictures that sear the imagination."
The Independent on Sunday

0-7445-3166-7   £5.99

MELISANDE
by E. Nesbit

The story of an unfortunate princess by the author of *The Railway Children* and *Five Children and It*.

"A joyfully funny fairy tale, illustrated with wit and traditional richness." *The Guardian*

0-7445-1485-1   £5.99

CATKIN
by Antonia Barber

Shortlisted for the Kate Greenaway Medal and Winner of the Bisto Irish Children's Book Award (Illustrator Category)

The enchanting story of a tiny cat called Catkin sent to bring back a human child from the magical Little People, who have taken her for their own.

"Barber is a superb storyteller and this tale … has the captivating quality of a fairy story handed down through generations. Richly illustrated by P. J. Lynch it is a joy to read aloud." *The Daily Telegraph*

0-7445-4768-7   £5.99